The Time Sailors

IAN WHYBROW

Illustrations by

ANTHONY LEWIS

WALKER BOOKS
AND SUBSIDIARIES
LONDON • BOSTON • SYDNEY

*To the memory of
my father, Ted,
and to my darling
Auntie Florrie*

First published 1994 by Walker Books Ltd
87 Vauxhall Walk, London SE11 5HJ

This edition published 1999

2 4 6 8 10 9 7 5 3 1

Text © 1994 Ian Whybrow
Illustrations © 1994 Anthony Lewis

This book has been typeset in Plantin.

Printed in England

British Library Cataloguing in Publication Data
A catalogue record for this book is
available from the British Library.

ISBN 0-7445-6381-X

Contents

Chapter 1

Captain Edward Coming Aboard

Edward crossed his fingers as he always did before he went up the three steps of number 23 Wren Terrace. He thrust his hands deep into the pockets of his anorak, and stood shivering in front of the door with the stained glass picture of a three-masted ship sailing into the sun. It wasn't just that he was a bit anxious by nature. No, the thing was, he was a long way from home. And besides, you never knew what to expect in this house.

He took a deep breath, leant forward and, rather than risk taking his hands out of his pockets, pressed the bell with his nose. It vibrated a bit but he couldn't hear if it rang, because of the roar of the Hoover. Edward knew that Grandad Wilson never bothered with hoovering. Great Aunt Spud must be in there, fussing away.

Edward turned his back to the door and looked down at the railings, at the flagstone path, at the row of Victorian houses all squashed together, at the cars parked nose-to-tail in the road. It was all so sad, somehow. Suddenly he was filled with panic and wanted to run away. He saw himself sprint back to the corner, jump on a bus heading for the station. It wouldn't take all that long on the train, back to New Eltham. He felt safe in New Eltham. He knew his way about in New Eltham, but not here in Greenwich. All he really knew about Greenwich was the way between this house – 23 Wren Terrace – and the station. And he'd been here by himself only – what, four times? Yes, four times since his Mum and Dad stopped visiting.

He tensed his muscles, ready to run. He could always say that he'd rung and rung and nobody had answered. Mum and Dad would probably believe him. They knew how awkward Grandad Wilson was. It was because he was so awkward that they'd fallen out with him. Now

Edward was his only family visitor – apart from Great Aunt Spud, Grandad Wilson's sister, and she quarrelled with him, too.

"I'm going," Edward said out loud. Before he could move, he heard a click and he sensed that the door had opened behind him. "Act casual, act casual," he told himself, taking his hands out of his pockets and pulling back the left sleeve to look at his watch. He gazed at his wrist for several seconds before he remembered he hadn't got a watch. He'd fallen off his bike and smashed it. Stupid, stupid.

The sound of the Hoover grew louder as the door inched wider. Edward smelt the familiar peppery mixture of geraniums, cat wee and coal smoke wafting over him in a warm cloud. He froze, feeling foolish, feeling watchful eyes on him.

A sudden shout, distant but sharp, made him jump. "Don't let that boy in the house with his street shoes on!" It was Great Aunt Spud all right, calling from the other end of the hall. The Hoover gasped its last breath as she added, "We don't want dogs' muck all over the carpet!" She had a thing about dogs' muck.

As she was speaking, Edward found himself staring into the whiskery face of his grandad. The old man was standing stiffly to attention in the narrow entrance. He winked and brought up his right hand in a smart salute. "Ship's company, stand by!" he said. Then he said, "Captain coming aboard!" and popped a bosun's whistle between his lips.

Wooo-EEEEE-ooo! went the whistle and Grandad Wilson motioned for the boy to enter. Edward stepped in, on to the red and black tiles among the tall potted plants, and immediately dropped on to one knee to undo the laces on his trainers.

"Take no notice of Spud, cocker," whispered Grandad Wilson. "Leave your nimbles on." He ducked his head and took guard with his clenched fists in front of his chin, like a boxer. "I fancy going a couple of rounds with her today, keep her on her toes."

Roger the cat slid out of the front room and

bumped Edward's backside with his fat head. Edward chucked him under the chin so that he rasped and dribbled with pleasure. He felt the tension draining out of him.

"Is Roger still doing squirts on the geraniums?" Edward grinned.

"Aye aye, cocker! He's an expert! Never been known to miss!" said Grandad Wilson with pride. "Come through to the back. We'll have the fight first and then we'll brew up."

"Edward! Your shoes!" protested Great Aunt Spud as he stepped down from the passage into the cosy little parlour. A glowing coal fire warmed the room. Great Aunt Spud was wearing a pinny over a track suit with a Blackheath Athletics Club badge.

"Don't fuss, Spud," said Grandad Wilson. "You worry too much about dogs' doings."

Great Aunt Spud's round, wrinkled face darkened. She shot her brother a savage look, switched off the ancient upright Hoover and made a dive for Edward's legs, lifting up one foot, then the other, like a blacksmith checking a horse's hooves. Arms like a blacksmith, too, thought Edward.

"Did you come Greenwich Park way, Edward?" she demanded. "I don't know what your mother was thinking of – letting a ten-year-old boy run about London on his own. There was a very nasty dog's job by the phone box on the corner and another one on the pavement just past the Chinese take-away. I nearly stepped in it myself while I was jogging."

"She's got 'em all mapped out!" sighed Grandad Wilson, running his fingers through his whiskers and smoothing down his droopy moustache. "Isn't it time you went home, girl? You've got this place shining like a dockyard ditty-box."

"I'll go when I've dusted and not before," snapped Great Aunt Spud, furiously winding up the flex on the Hoover. "*You* may have lowered your standards since Emily passed away but I have not." To show she meant business, she whipped her duster out from under her pinny-belt and snatched the photo of Edward's long-dead grandmother off the mantelpiece. "She must be turning in her grave," she said, holding it out to accuse them. But there was no sign of irritation in the face of Grandma Wilson. She only smiled at them in her coat with the big shoulders and waved a bunch of bluebells. Great Aunt Spud gave her a good going over with the cloth.

Edward took off his anorak and toasted the back of his legs by the fire while Great Aunt Spud danced about, flicking and jabbing with her duster. She barged Edward to one side to have a go at Grandad Wilson's naval officer's sword hanging in its scabbard on the chimney breast. *Flick-flack*. Then she was in among the bits on his sideboard – *swish-swash* – thrashing the black wooden elephant-lamp with one ivory tusk missing. *Blit-blat* – she attacked the row of books on navigation. *Whick-whack*. That was for the Chinese box with the secret drawers. *Biff-baff*. Another one for the wooden parrot that swung on its perch when

you pushed its tail. *Crick-crack*. One for
the model of a schooner that Grandad
Wilson had rescued from his cabin on
HMS *Southampton*, the night the ship was
torpedoed. One, two – *jab-jab*.

She was really moving now, bobbing and
weaving, getting herself nicely balanced for a
good smack at Edward's two favourite things:
the fat silver pocket watch that he mustn't
touch, and the fading brown photo of two
serious boys and a baby in an old-fashioned
pram. Grandad Wilson wasn't having that.
"Leave those!" he shouted and made
Edward jump.

Great Aunt Spud froze for a moment, but
she was obviously collecting her strength.

"Don't you touch those," Grandad Wilson
said, quieter but still determined.

"Awkward!" said Great Aunt Spud
furiously, spinning round to face him.
"Awkward, that's what you are, Ernie Wilson.
And if it wasn't for me keeping you clean and
tidy, you'd be up to your neck in muck and

disorder!" She tipped her head towards Edward. "You certainly wouldn't get *his* mother round here, clearing up after you. She'd have you in a Home and no mistake!"

Edward didn't know where to look. It was true. He'd heard his mother say as much. She and his dad could hardly bear to be in the same room with Grandad Wilson. Edward was the only person who got on with him at all.

"Shove off back to your own house! Sling your hook!" shouted Grandad Wilson.

"I shall!" said Great Aunt Spud, punching the cushion in the big armchair into shape on her way to the hall. "But not before I've given the rest of the house a proper going over." She slammed the Hoover into the cupboard under the stairs and armed herself with a feather duster. Roger wound round her legs and she pushed him away roughly. "And you want to have this cat seen to. It's unhygienic, the way he goes around spraying everything."

"I'll have the vet see to *you* before he lays a finger on Roger!" said Grandad Wilson.

"Take no notice of him, Edward, he's showing off," said Great Aunt Spud with dignity. "I shall carry on upstairs. I expect no thanks."

"And you won't get any!" Grandad Wilson had the last word, but before Great Aunt Spud went upstairs, she banged the door to the front room so hard that hot coals spilled out of the fire and made the rug smoulder.

Chapter 2

Home Truths

"What do you want to keep fighting with her for?" asked Edward. His grandad pushed the red hot coals back on to the grate with his toe and scuffed out the smoking bits on the rug.

"She likes it," he said. "What else are sisters for? Besides, I wanted to spend some time with you without having her buzzing about in here like a blue-arsed fly."

Edward thought of his own sister, Pinkie – how they sat in front of the telly sometimes, not saying anything, just pinching each other till their arms were black. Other times they got on OK.

"She's a rare old party, Spud," said Grandad Wilson. "I think the world of her – though don't you go blabbing to her I said so. She's coming up for eighty and I'm well past that now. How else am I supposed to keep us both on the go? The only reason she stays in training is so she can keep pace with me. And it's no good relying on *your* family to keep our blood pumping round, is it? Your lot are scared stiff of the pair of us!"

"No, they're not," said Edward, rising to their defence. "They just think you're gaga."

Grandad Wilson stiffened. He snatched up the poker and stabbed it into the fire so that sparks flew and a cloud of smoke puffed into the room. "So that's what they say, is it? That's very nice, that is – talking like that about me behind my back, saying I'm gaga. What else do they say about me?"

Edward wished he'd kept his mouth shut now, but it was too late. He might as well come out with it all. "Well, you won't have a telly. And you won't have Roger seen to and you shout at people. And you never say please or thank you and you won't let anybody help you except Aunt Spud and she's too old. And you'd be better off in a Home. That's what they think."

Edward waited for his grandad to explode, to tell him to sling his hook.

"Won't have a telly!" roared Grandad Wilson, riddling the coals so that they cracked and spat. "I don't *need* a telly! I've got better things to do with my time. Since when has not having a telly been a sign of madness?"

"I just can't see why you never say thank you to anybody, no matter what they do for you," said Edward bluntly. "That's what puts people off."

"I do. Inside," murmured Grandad Wilson.

"Well, why don't you try saying it out loud just once in a while?"

"I can't..." said Grandad Wilson. Then he added urgently, "There's a reason. But I can't tell you, not when I gave my word not to. I could take you with me and *show* you, maybe, if things worked out..."

What's he talking about? Edward thought. *Take me where? He's too old to go anywhere. And show me what? Maybe he* is *bonkers.*

"...but before we shove off, I've got to be

really certain I can trust you."

"Thanks a bunch," said Edward.

"Trouble is, cocker, you think I'm round the bend, too, don't you?"

"Don't know," said Edward. He couldn't honestly say he didn't. He couldn't think of anybody who behaved quite like his grandad.

"But at least it doesn't bother you, does it?"

Edward shook his head. It was true. He didn't care if Grandad Wilson *was* round the bend. He liked being with him.

"Well, that's all right then," said Grandad Wilson, suddenly grinning from ear to ear. "At least I've got *you* on my side. You hungry?"

"Starving!" said Edward.

"Goodo! If you and I are going to catch the tide later on, we'd better build up a head of steam. Fancy a fry-up?"

They had the fry-up on the fire. Grandad Wilson said he couldn't get on with the gas stove. There was a black metal plate on a hinge, called a trivet. You swung it over the fire and you could stand the frying pan on it.

"Sling the fat dobs in the pan first," Grandad Wilson said, pointing to the bacon. "Then we'll do the whistlers in the grease."

"You mean the eggs?" Edward smiled.

"What else?" said Grandad Wilson.

"Well, you could have meant the bread," said Edward.

"No, no, whistlers are eggs. Stungee's the Navy word for bread," said Grandad Wilson. "And I reckon stungee's better toasted. I'll do that. You take charge of the fry-up." He reached for a long-handled brass toasting fork and plugged a thick wodge of bread on it.

"I don't think I'd be any good at frying," Edward confessed. "I've never really done cooking before."

"You'll manage," said Grandad Wilson. "Just give yourself a chance. It's as easy as rowing a boat."

Edward pushed the sizzling bacon about with a fork to stop it sticking to the bottom of the pan. Some of the fat went into the fire and made it flare up. Grandad Wilson told him not to worry, it happened all the time.

"Now let's be doing this all shipshape and Bristol-fashion," he said. "I'll have my whistler sunny-side up. Can you manage that?"

Edward wasn't sure about cracking eggs into a pan, but Grandad Wilson told him to have a go and he did. At first he was too gentle, but then he gave it a good knock on the side of the pan so that the shell split. Most of the egg went into the pan all right, but it was a bit mashed up. "I'll have that one," he said. "I'll do better with the next one. Watch!" He took his time with the second egg, making a cleaner cut in the shell, opening it up closer to the pan.

"Stap me, that's perfect!" yelled Grandad Wilson as the white began to form around the unbroken yellow yolk. "Tiddly job, cocker! Now all we need is a couple of mugs of Rosy Lea."

They had their tea with condensed milk. It tasted more interesting than ordinary tea, strong and sweet, and the good thing was, you could get the condensed milk up off the bottom of your mug with a spoon and eat it warm.

Edward was just wiping round his plate with his last chunk of thick buttery toast when his eye was drawn to the things on the sideboard. The lovely untouchable silver pocket watch had never looked more smooth and shiny. And there was something more fascinating than ever about the faded brown photograph in the leather frame.

Two skinny boys stared out, concentrating hard. Each had an arm round the other's shoulder. The taller lad with the cropped fair hair was holding up an oar with his free hand. That was Grandad Wilson. The other, the one with a hank of dark hair hanging limp over his right eye, had his hand on the handle of a big old-fashioned pram. That was Futter. Behind them, there was a river, with lots of ships – sailing ships, some of them, a bit like pirate ships, because this was in the olden days, round about 1919.

And the thing that had always puzzled Edward was the cap. There was a cap, an old-fashioned cloth cap, that seemed to be just floating in the air between young Grandad Wilson and his friend, at a level with the handle of the pram. If there had been a sudden gust of wind that tossed it up from the ground, how come Futter's hair was just hanging down limp? Edward had often asked Grandad Wilson about this mystery, but he would never go into details. When the time was ripe, Edward would find out, he would say. When the time was ripe and not before. What did that mean, ripe? How could you have ripe time?

"Why wouldn't you let Aunt Spud dust those things, Grandad?" he said, his buttery thumb indicating the pocket watch and the photo.

"So you noticed that, did you? Good. Shows you keep your eyes peeled. A good sign, that. Shows you're interested. We're moving in the right direction here. Good lad."

"What does that mean – 'moving in the right direction'?" asked Edward.

"Means you might have what it takes to steer some tricky waters. Means I might let you into my secret."

Edward knew better than to beg to be let into a secret. He knew that people with secrets liked to tease you with them, so he changed the subject. "Tell me about Futter," he said.

A cunning look came over Grandad Wilson's face. "Futter? Who's Futter?"

"Come on, Grandad. That's Futter in the photo with his hair in his eyes, holding on to the pram. And the other one's you. You've told me that loads of times."

"Have I...?"

Was Grandad Wilson teasing or testing?

"And you said you and Futter always used to muck about together when you were kids – in the olden days."

"Ah, the olden days," echoed Grandad Wilson. "You make it sound like B.C. or something! But I'll tell you when it was.

B.T., I call it – Before Television. Stap me, we knew how to enjoy ourselves then!" He rubbed his leathery hands till they whistled.

"Doing what?"

"All sorts."

"Like what? You say you had a good time, but you never say doing what."

"You'd really like to know, wouldn't you?"

"Yes, I really would. He was a good mate, wasn't he – Futter?"

"Best oppo ever. Never be another like him," said Grandad Wilson firmly. "Had guts, he did. And he knew how to keep his word."

Edward was hurt. Jealous maybe. "What about me?" he said. "Aren't I your mate? Don't I come round to see you whenever I can? And who is it sticks up for you when Mum and Dad say you're going daft and not fit to be living on your own!"

"So you stick up for a crazy old barnacle like me, do you, eh?" said Grandad Wilson.

"Course I do," said Edward.

Grandad Wilson got rapidly to his feet and

plonked his empty plate on the mantelpiece. "What's the time now?" he said.

Automatically, Edward looked at his wrist before he remembered. "Haven't got a watch," he said.

"Oh, yes you have," said Grandad Wilson, his pale blue eyes shining. He reached over to the sideboard and picked up the silver pocket watch. He held it in the flat of his large hand for a second, looking at it thoughtfully, as if it were a frog or a small bird. Then he turned and held it towards his grandson. "The time's just about ripe, I reckon," he said. "We're off!"

"What?" said Edward stupidly because he suddenly felt his skin prickle with a wave of half-fearful pleasure.

"Take it," said Grandad Wilson firmly. "It's for you."

Chapter 3

The Cupboard Under the Stairs

....

The watch felt heavy and smooth in Edward's hand. And though he couldn't hear it when he pressed it to his ear, it seemed to him that it was ticking gently. If they had babies this small, he was thinking, they would feel like this. This was something precious. And now it was his.

In the centre of its silver case, there was a glass disc through which you could see the hands and the figures. The hands were set at twelve. That was wrong, surely.

"Is it working, Grandad?" Edward asked.

"Oh yes, it's working."

"How do you wind it?"

"No need. Just hold it firm, let the watch do the rest. You all set?"

"Set for what?"

"To catch the tide. We're going on a little

cruise, you and I." He started moving towards the front door but stopped by the cupboard under the stairs.

Edward thought for a moment that the old man had stopped to catch his breath. That made him worry about whether he could manage him on his own, once they were out of the house.

But Grandad Wilson was turning the brass handle on the cupboard door. "In here," he said. "This way." He opened the door with its slanting top, ducked his head and stepped in.

"What's this – hide-and-seek?" said Edward with rather a nervous laugh. When he got no reply, he peered into the gloom, at the dusty shelves lined with crumbly old paper, at the dusty brushes and jars and boxes. He couldn't see his grandad at all.

"Where are you?" he called, and found that his voice echoed. He pushed past the old Hoover with the bag hanging on a spring that went *tang-tang*. Then he eased round some lumpy piled-up bundles of newspaper, keeping his head on one side to avoid banging it on the stairs. "Are you there?" he called again. The cupboard was deeper than he'd thought. Much deeper.

"See if any of those fit," he heard Grandad Wilson say from somewhere ahead. Looking to his left, Edward could dimly make out a row of pegs with hats hanging.

Not dressing up, surely! thought Edward, a bit annoyed with his grandad for trying to get him to play some babyish game. Still, no harm in humouring him. There was a naval seaman's cap, a straw boater, a mouldy topper, a broad-brimmed trilby and a dusty round bowler. They were all miles too big for Edward, flopping down over his ears. There was a rubber gas mask, too, hanging by its strap, and when Edward tried it on, it sounded like waves breaking on the shingle at Herne Bay. "What about this?" he called in a voice that was muffled through the strange snout at the front.

"Another time, maybe, but no need for gas masks today."

It was so difficult to see, Edward thought. How could he choose when it was so dim? "Is there a light here, Grandad?" Edward said.

"Don't worry about the darkness. It'll be light soon enough," said Grandad Wilson. "Once you've found the hat that fits, we'll be ready to cast off."

"Where are we going?" Edward asked, trying to keep the impatience out of his voice. Honestly, this was a bit stupid. He transferred the watch to his left hand for a second, reached up with his right and felt rough cloth – and the stiff peak of a cap. He plopped it on to his head, expecting it to be as big and silly as the others, but he found it fitted him exactly. "This one fits me," he said.

"Then that's the one and we've got all we need," said Grandad Wilson. "Now we can put you in the picture. You'd like to be in the picture, wouldn't you?"

"I don't get it, Grandad."

"It's dead simple," said Grandad Wilson. "We're going to see Futter."

Edward had no time to do anything apart from open his mouth in astonishment. No sooner was the cap on his head than the watch in his hand grew hot. "Ouch!" he yelled, not hurt, but startled.

"Don't drop the watch, whatever you do!" called Grandad Wilson. "Hang on tight to it and give me your other hand. Trust me."

It was like holding a hot potato or a newly boiled egg, but Edward clung on and reached out for his grandad's fingers. As soon as he touched them with his own, a great surging shock went through him, starting from the watch and flowing along his outstretched arms like an electric charge. Suddenly, he was aware that the watch was pumping like a living heart! He looked down at it and saw that it was a glowing, pulsing ball of blue fire. He turned his head then, and to his amazement he saw that every whisker, every visible hair on

Grandad Wilson's face and head was crackling with dancing blue sparks.

"Don't look at me. Concentrate on the watch, and listen! There are going to be some changes, but you'll get used to them. You'll seem just normal to other people, so don't panic if you can't see your reflection anywhere. Stick with me and you'll be fine. When we get there, stow the watch in your pocket. Then hang on to me till you hear the horse. That'll be the start of the sequence. Hold on tight, now! Watch the hands! Brace yourself!" urged Grandad Wilson.

It took all Edward's courage to do as he was told and he saw that the hands of the watch, now glowing red against the blue, were beginning to move – backwards. At first they revolved slowly, and then faster and faster.

Suddenly, a cold wind came roaring out of the darkness, lifting Edward and his grandad into the air like dry leaves. Edward was terrified. He kicked out to try to steady himself.

"Don't jib!" yelled Grandad Wilson, tugging at his hand. "Sail before the wind! When you're caught in a squall, you must ride it out!"

Once Edward had let the wind take him, his terror left him. How long he was sailing through the darkness he had no idea, but it was long enough for him to begin to enjoy the feeling of weightlessness. He came to land almost without realizing it, and found himself walking in a place that was steadily growing less dark.

"Catch hold of my collar now, and follow me," said a voice. It was Grandad Wilson's voice, and yet it wasn't. It was lighter, not so gruff, younger somehow. Edward did as he was told and let himself be guided along what seemed to be a gloomy, echoing tunnel. He was surprised by how awkward and heavy his trainers felt – as if they weren't trainers at all, but great clumsy boots. And the noise they made on the hard floor!

"Quiet!" said Grandad Wilson. *Was* that

Grandad Wilson's voice? "Don't scuff the tiles or my ma'll skin you!"

There was a familiar peppery smell in the air. It puzzled Edward. Surely they'd gone quite the wrong way to be approaching Grandad Wilson's front door. And yet, there was light ahead, shining through the top half of a door. Straining his eyes, he could make out the coloured glass, and the pattern of a stained glass ship sailing into the sun. What's more, there was enough light to show Edward the silhouette of the figure in front of him. His heart began to race even more wildly as he realized that the collar he was holding was no higher than his own. The shadowy figure wasn't an old man at all, but a stranger – a strange *boy*!

It was a horrible shock.

"Grandad!" screamed Edward. "Grandad, where are you?"

"Pipe down!" hissed the boy. He was tallish – just a little taller than Edward – and skinny, maybe ten or eleven. His hair, Edward could now clearly see, was bright red and looked as though it had been cropped with kitchen scissors. "You'll wake the baby!" the boy whispered. "And leave go of my collar, will you? You're strangling me!"

Edward let go. "Have we arrived?" he said nervously.

"Arrived? We ain't started yet, cocker, and if you wake young Spuddy, we'll be stuck inside all day looking after her," replied the boy. "So pipe down."

The word "cocker" made a voice stir in Edward's head. It was a gruff voice saying, "There are going to be some changes... You'll get used to them... Don't panic..." He decided that the time had come for him to put the watch safely into his jeans pocket. But when he reached down, he discovered another peculiar thing. He wasn't wearing jeans any more. He was dressed in a pair of baggy short trousers made of prickly cloth. They came up almost to his chest, held in place by thick braces fastened to buttons on the front and back, and they came down to just below his knees. There was only one pocket, on the right-hand side, a deep one. He slid the watch into it, and stood absolutely still in the dim passage, holding his breath while he listened. He listened so hard, his ears started to whistle. At last, there was a sound, the *clip-clop* of hooves on a stony road and the squeak and scrape of iron wheels against a kerbstone.

"Blast, it's the coalman!" said the boy. "That's torn it. Ma's bound to have heard him. Quick, let's get outside before she realizes we're here and finds us a job!"

They clattered (Edward could see now that he *was* wearing thick old boots) over the red and black tiles along the passage to the narrow entrance hall, where their way was blocked by an enormous old pram. Squeezing past, they were forced to brush against the leaves of two or three huge potted geranium plants and the air was filled with their scent as the red-headed boy cautiously pulled open the door with the stained glass window. They tiptoed down the three steps, on to the pavement.

And there they almost collided with the coalman, grinning white teeth and white eyes out of his black face. Behind him his sturdy brown horse blinked and snuffled between the shafts of the filthy cart. Coal dust drifted from the man's leather apron as he backed up against the coal cart. He felt with his right arm and grabbed the neck of the heavy sack, stooped, and pulled it on to his head and shoulder in one quick movement. The horse shook itself like a wet dog and its harness slapped and tinkled.

"Hundredweight for number 23?" the coalman said to Edward. Edward looked at the underfed kid at his side for the answer. The boy wiped his nose on the sleeve of his ragged pullover and grunted yes. The coalman pushed open the side gate with his shoulder. "Round the back or dahn the chute, chummy?" he said.

"Down the chute," said the boy and the

coalman called, "Git on, Jimmy!" The horse ducked its head and heaved the cart along the kerb until it was level with the coal-hole in the pavement.

"Ernie!" came a woman's loud voice. "Ernie! Where is the little perisher?" It was coming from inside the house. Edward noticed as he turned that the lace of one of his heavy boots had come undone and he dropped on to one knee to tie it. As he bent over, he felt his braces pulling at his shoulders and a sudden cold draught through a hole in the seat of his short pants. He was feeling the place where the coarse material had worn thin when the door he had just come through was whipped open. A tall, stern, red-haired woman in a long black dress stood there holding out a baby in a dark blue smock. "Don't you sneak off without taking Florry!" she said. "Or I'll fetch you one, Ernie Wilson! Now give me a hand down with the pram."

Glumly, Ernie Wilson climbed the steps and prepared to bump the clumsy great pram down to the pavement.

"You!" said Ernie's mother, holding out the baby to Edward. "Make yourself a bit useful, whoever you are. Hold Florry." And Edward took the baby over his shoulder and felt it dribble down his neck.

When young Florry was strapped in, and Ernie's mother had rustled back indoors, the baby lifted her arm and wiggled her fingers to show that she wanted to touch the horse. The coalman bent double and shot the sack full of coal down the hole, where it grumbled and crashed. He folded it over his arm and tossed it on to the pile of empty sacks at the back of the coal cart. "Hup, Jimmy!" he shouted, and the horse dipped its head and started to pull forward just as Florry touched its mane with her fingers. She bubbled with laughter.

Ernie shook the pram up and down by the handle to make the laugh last longer and then raced down the street, with the baby bouncing and enjoying herself. When Edward caught up with them, they'd got as far as the gas lamp at the top of the road. Florry did a sick down her front. It wasn't much, so Ernie wiped it off on the covers. The baby smiled, pulling her funny little face into a lumpy shape.

"Look at her little fizzog!" laughed Ernie. "Makes you smile when she does that, don't she! I call her our Little Spud-Face, I do. Don't I, Spuddy?" He jiggled his fingers under Florry's chin and the baby went "*Kuh-kuh-kuh-kuh-kuh*". Ernie admired her for a moment before turning to Edward, who was also enjoying the show. "Let's go down Standing's Yard," Ernie said.

"Down where?" said Edward.

"Down the river," said Ernie. "Then maybe we'll row along to Deptford Creek if the tide's right. Depends if we can get a borrow of a boat."

"I'm not allowed on the river," said Edward uneasily.

Ernie didn't seem to hear him. "We'd better hurry up," he said. "Futter'll think we ain't coming!"

Chapter 4

Futter

....

"Do I know Futter?" panted Edward as he rushed to keep up with Ernie. Ernie didn't seem to hear him. They'd come down Vanburgh Hill to where they could see across Trafalgar Road to Blackwall Lane. The granite chippings in the road gave way to sticky tar blocks and tramlines. Here there were dozens of horse-drawn carts and wagons and noisy old motor vans. A tram clattered towards them with a sign on the front that said GREENWICH PARK AND HIGH ROAD. It went by with a thunderous, grinding roar and a bell *ding-dong*ing, shaking the ground where they stood. Edward could see Ernie and the pram reflected in the flashing windows, but he must have been standing at an odd angle or something, because all he could see of himself was his cap – just floating in the air.

"Come on!" urged Ernie and he shoved the pram out on to the tar blocks while there was a gap in the traffic. They crossed the road, crashing the baby over the tram tracks, and turned left.

They reached Romney Road, where tall cast-iron railings ran as far as the eye could see, with a thick privet hedge behind. Through it, the boys caught glimpses of a parade ground and great stone buildings beyond.

"The Royal Hospital School, Greenwich!" announced Ernie proudly. "I'm going there when I'm eleven. I'm going to take a scholarship and be a Boreman Boy. They give you your sailor's uniform … free. You don't have to pay for it or nothing. And they have these special boots with straps coming across the front. Smashing. Then, when I'm fourteen, I'm joining the Royal Navy with George Fell and Futter. Look at that!"

They had reached the enormous double entrance gates. Two boys in naval uniform, just as Ernie had described, were standing in the sentry box. Behind them, dwarfing them completely, loomed the three incredibly tall masts of a great sailing ship that was set into the concrete.

"Man o' War – *Fame*," declared Ernie. "Every morning, crack of dawn, you have to climb the rigging to the masthead. Me and George and Futter, we're going to be button boys – that's what they call you when you stand right on top of the mast!"

"Sooner you than me," said Edward. Just looking up there made him feel dizzy. As they wandered on, Edward asked his question again. "Who's Futter?" He knew the name from somewhere.

"His dad's a copper," Ernie said. "Futter knows everybody round here, Harbour Master and all. He's talking to him about borrowing the boat right now."

"Er – I'm not really allowed on the river," said Edward for the second time.

"Nor am I, but you'll be all right with me," said Ernie, and he seemed so sure that

Edward felt less bad about it.

They were near the river now. One way, the Royal Hospital School way, you could see past Greenwich Pier and Ernie said that where all the cranes were was Deptford. The other way was Piper's Wharf, some long, low buildings by the bargeworks, and the generating station. Beyond that, Ernie pointed out, was the wireworks where they made ships' cables and the dog biscuit factory they called the Molathene.

"Is that a park over there, across the river?" Edward asked.

"Yeah, they have swings – even a roundabout!" said Ernie, as though it was something really special. "We could walk there later through the Foot Tunnel if you like. Little Spud likes going in the lifts."

Edward felt confused. There were so many things about this area that seemed different somehow. *Walk* through a tunnel? Hadn't he driven with his dad through a tunnel under the river and come along Park Row, where they were now? And yet now he couldn't see a single car.

The ground by the Harbour Master's hut was rough, all cobbles. Florry laughed like mad and went "*Uh-uh-uh-uh-uh-uh-uh*" over the bumps. A boy with bloody knees and holes in the elbows of his jumper leapt out of the Harbour Master's hut to greet them. He looked at the pram, put his hands on his hips and grinned. A hank of jet black hair flopped over his right eye.

"Don't you start taking the rise about me bringing Spuddy!" warned Ernie. "Or I'll beat your head in, Futter."

Futter didn't say anything except, "Who's he?"

Ernie put his finger on his nose. "Keep it out, Futter," he said. "Ask no questions and I'll tell you no lies."

"Is he in the Dare Gang?" asked Futter, pushing his hair back.

"Might be," said Ernie. "Eh, Edward?" He winked at Edward.

"What's happened to your knees?" Edward asked Futter.

Futter touched one with his dirty fingers and licked the blood. "Climbing over the wall by the bargeworks. Why?"

"Did you get a boat?" interrupted Ernie.

"Course I did!" said Futter. "She's moored down that way. Done a good one yesterday."

"Good what?" asked Ernie, adding, "Here, chum, you can push for a bit." Futter flicked back his hair and looked at the baby. Little Spud lifted her arm with her finger pointing at Futter and said, "Dad-dad-dad-dad-dad!"

"No, I ain't!" said Futter, laughing. He went on, as he pushed the pram over the cobbles. "Yes, I done a good dare yesterday."

"What'd you do, Futter – cross the road?" mocked Ernie.

"Funny-ha-ha," said Futter. "If you must know, I dived into a barge full of water. George Fell seen me do it."

"Where from?" said Ernie.

"Off the harbour wall. Tide was out, too. It

was a heck of a way down. Bet you wouldn't do it!"

Ernie kept walking. "How much?"

"Sportsman's bet."

"I'm only doing it for money. How much you got?"

Futter reached into the pocket of his ragged trousers and dug out two coins, one big brown one and another half its size. "Penny ha'penny," he said. "But me mum wants a penny change."

"Well, I ain't risking my neck for a ha'penny," Ernie said. He turned to Edward. "How much you got, cocker?"

Edward felt in his pocket, down past the smoothness of the watch, to the pointy bit right at the bottom. There among the fluff he located a small coin with a rough edge to it. Edward brought it into the daylight and read "Sixpence" on its silver side.

Futter let go of the pram with one hand and slapped it under Edward's open palm, so that the coin shot up in the air and he was able to snatch it. "Blimey! Look at that – a tanner!

Where'd you pinch that from?"

"You didn't pinch it, did you?" asked Ernie, looking serious. "'Cos that's one of our rules, that is. The Dare Gang never pinches, never splits, never breaks a promise."

"I didn't know I had it," said Edward. "I just found it in my pocket. Keep it if you want it."

Futter couldn't believe his ears. "Cor! Has he got a screw loose or something – giving good money away?" he said and passed the coin to Ernie, who said it was more than he could save in a month. While they were discussing the sixpence, the baby started to cry. She couldn't half cry, and the boys didn't know what to do about it. Ernie took the coin from Futter and handed it back to Edward, telling him to put it away and keep it safe. Futter bounced the pram hard, up and down on its curving springs, until Florry's face turned into a smiley potato again. But as soon as the movement stopped, she was off again, crying louder than ever.

"You'd better see if she's done anything," suggested Futter. Ernie stuck his head in the pram, sniffed and said he couldn't smell anything. "Prob'ly hungry then," Futter said.

Ernie rummaged about among the blankets and came up with a glass bottle wrapped in a spare nappy. Florry switched to a different noise. Ernie bent the rubber teat against the back of his hand and a bit of milk squidged out. "Warm," he said.

"Blood heat?" asked Futter.

"What are you, an expert?" said Ernie and shoved the teat into Florry's mouth. Peace at last. *"Gung, gung, gung,"* went Florry and the boys set off again, Futter still pushing.

"Sunnink else in here," Futter said, squeezing his hand down where Ernie had found the bottle. He came up with a thick wedge of something wrapped in greaseproof paper.

"Leave off!" threatened Ernie. "That'll be a nice chunk of bread pudding for my dinner."

"Go on, gi's a bit, Ernie," pleaded Futter. "I got us a boat, didn't I?"

"I might give you a bit when we get in the boat," Ernie agreed grudgingly. It wasn't long before they had trudged down-river of the generating station to some stone steps. Below them, nicely varnished and tied by a rope to a ring set into the riverside wall, bobbed a three-seater rowing-boat.

Ernie unstrapped the baby, who was coming to the end of her milk. He lifted her up and sat her on his arm. "Err!" he said, turning up his nose. "She's done one!"

"*Errrp!*" said Florry.

"Now she's done anuvver one!" laughed Futter.

"I'm not talking about her foghorn. I'm talking about below decks," laughed Ernie, joining in the fun. He presented Florry's stern section for Futter to inspect. When Futter jumped back three paces with a yell of disgust, it was pretty obvious that something had to be seen to.

"Edward, my old mucker," said Futter, clasping his nostrils firmly between finger and thumb. "Fetch her spare nappy over here." When Edward had supplied what was asked for, Futter let go of his nose, took a deep breath and said to Ernie, "Give her me, I'll change her."

"No fear!" said Ernie protectively. "She's my sister, cocker!" And he laid her down on some grass. Florry stopped screaming when the mucky nappy came off but when Ernie tried to get the new one on her, she started up again. "Now what?" said Ernie, looking a bit desperate.

"Leave it," said Futter. "Bring the spare nappy with you. She'll calm down when we get her in the boat."

Nobody was quite sure what to do with the smelly nappy. Futter suggested chucking it into the Thames, but Ernie said that his mum would give him a hiding if he didn't take it home. "Well, at least give it a bit of a wash in the water," pleaded Futter. "It don't half pong."

Ernie said he didn't want to risk it because they were strictly forbidden to go near the river, so they'd have to put up with it niffing a bit. It was Edward's idea to wrap it in the greaseproof paper, and Ernie let him hold the baby while he divided the bread pudding into three. Then he wrapped up the dirty nappy and stuck it under the blanket in the pram. After that, the boys filled their cheeks with bread pudding. It was crunchy on the outside, but soggy enough in the middle for them to be able to quieten the baby with little bits to suck. Edward wished it was sweeter and he thought at first he might spit it out. But when he saw how eagerly Ernie and Futter were munching their share, he changed his mind and swallowed it.

When it was all gone, Ernie licked round his chops so as not to waste a crumb. Florry wasn't keen on bread pudding, it turned out, and started grizzling again. "Only one thing for it – whizz her round in the whirlpool," said Ernie. "All aboard!"

"Ship's company, stand by!" shouted Futter, scrambling down the steps and standing to attention. "Captain coming aboard!" He saluted smartly, then pursed his lips and made a sound like a bosun's whistle – "*Wooo-EEEEE-ooo!*"

Chapter 5

The Whirlpools

Futter sat in the stern and Ernie passed Florry to him before he climbed aboard the rowing-boat himself. When they'd settled her so that she was sitting on the floor in the middle of the boat on her spare nappy, wedged by her pillow against the centre seat, she was still howling.

"Get in and cast off," Ernie said to Edward. "But don't let go of the mooring ring until you're balanced. That's it." Edward began to wind up the rope. "Coil that painter and stow it nice and neat," said Ernie.

So you call the rope a painter, Edward thought. He settled himself in the bow seat without rocking the boat too much, tucking the painter out of the way, and shoved off from the steps. "What about the pram?" he said.

"That'll be fine till we get back," Futter said, taking hold of the tiller from his seat in the stern. "Full steam ahead!"

Ernie pulled strongly on one oar and the boat swung sharply round. "We'll head for the Isle of Dogs and let the tide bring us round," Ernie said. Soon they were gliding along smoothly out into the middle of the river, and drifting in the direction of the generating station. Florry's lung-power was amazing. She carried on bawling.

Gradually, the sound she made was half-smothered by a low, grumbling roar. Edward looked over his shoulder and what he saw made him very nervous indeed. There were two huge brick tunnels projecting out from the generating station. Edward reckoned they were about four or five metres apart. They were the housing for two massive iron pipes that ran quite a way out into the river. Something was spewing out of the end of the pipes that made the water thresh and boil and race round and round like the contents of two gigantic washing-machines. "What's that coming out of those pipes?" he yelled.

"Only hot water. It's the outflow from the

cooling system for the generating station."
Futter grinned. "They pump in cold water
and when it gets too hot, they pump it back
into the river through those pipes – tons of it.
See the steam rising? Comes out at a heck of a
rate, don't it? Listen to it churn!"

"Bring her round a bit on the tiller, Futter!"
yelled Ernie above the increasing noise.

"Not that way, Futter! You'll have us in one
of those whirlpools!" shouted Edward.

"Hold your course, Futter," called Ernie,
pulling harder than ever on both oars, and not
even turning his head to see the danger.
"Little Spud's been looking forward to this!"

"Ernie! You'll have us over!"

But Ernie took no notice and rowed for all
he was worth until the bow of the little craft
nudged the outer circle of the nearest
whirlpool. She began to plunge and dip wildly,
and then steadied for a second as she was
drawn along the rim of the giant saucer.

"Brace yourselves, everybody!" screamed
Ernie.

Suddenly, as if she'd been lassoed by a man on a galloping pony, the boat was gripped by a mighty force and whipped round like cake mixture in a bowl!

"Whee!" shrieked Edward and Futter with the terrifying pleasure of it. And as for Florry, gripped between Ernie's knees – she had closed her eyes as she was whisked round and round in wild and dizzying circles and was laughing her little head off!

"Listen to little Spud!" cried Ernie. "I told you a go on the roundabout would cheer her up! Wahoooo!" He threw back his head to get the most out of the wonderful giddiness of the ride.

A Dutch barge drifted past, red sails limp in the light air. "Ahoy! Ahoy!" yelled the boys, wanting to share the moment, but there seemed to be no one on deck to pay attention to them.

Across the river, however, somebody *was* paying attention, though the boys didn't see the sun glint on his binoculars. They were aware of the splutter of a motor long before they realized it was bearing down on them. It was Futter who eventually raised the alarm. "Police!" he mouthed, instinctively ducking down but finding nowhere to hide in the shallow boat. "Ernie, it's the River Police. We're for it now – and when my dad finds out, he'll take his belt to me."

Ernie was as calm as ever. "Shame we never brought a spare nappy for *you*, Futter. You could have stuck it on your head and disguised yourself as the Sheik of Araby," he snorted.

In his panic, Futter tried to lie flat. "Sit up, Futter," said Ernie. "Don't let them see you're in a muck sweat. We ain't broken no laws."

At a distance of thirty metres from the rowing-boat, the motor of the police boat was suddenly silenced. One policeman ran a stout pair of oars into the rowlocks and began to pull against the rising tide that ran stronger towards the middle of the river. The other policeman, seated in the stern behind the engine-hatch, called out through the cone-shaped loudhailer.

"Damn silly spot of bother you've got yourselves into, you boys. And isn't that young Futter? Well, I'm blowed! I should have thought you'd have more sense. Your father'll have a word or two to say to you when we get you ashore, and no mistake! Now – keep calm, don't panic, and we'll get a tow-rope to you."

The man at the oars bent to his job, but the boat was heavy and he was making painfully slow progress.

Ernie called out, "Don't trouble about us, sir. We're quite all right, sir. We're safe as houses, honest! We know what we're about."

"Don't you believe it, sonny Jim," called the policeman with the loudhailer. Turning to his sweating mate, he called, "Shall I give the motor a couple of turns?"

You could see the veins bulging under the tight collar of the policeman at the oars. His face was purple with strain. He was struggling to make any headway at all against the quickening criss-cross of black water. In fact, he was drifting back towards the other hot water outlet while Ernie and his companions twizzled happily in their whirlpool. His head was turned so that he could watch one of the chimneys of the generating station to give him something by which he could measure his progress while his mate was busy fiddling with the crank.

"I wouldn't row that way, sir, if I was you," warned Futter.

The oarsman told him not to be saucy.

"Well, you ain't me, young shaver," he panted. "And if you was, you wouldn't find yourself in your present pickle!"

"Watch out for the other— " yelled Ernie. He was going to say "whirlpool" but he was interrupted.

"I'll give you 'Watch out!'" raged the policeman who was struggling to start the engine. He reached behind him and tweaked the tiller a touch harder to port. As the blunt bow of the heavy police boat bent round with the current, he cranked harder and harder at the starting handle. Nothing happened. The purple-faced oarsman dug in his oars, but he was wasting his time. Even the longest, toughest arms of the law were no match for that tug-of-water. In a twitch, just the tick of a watch, the boat was caught by the tug of the twin whirlpool. That was it. Round and round she went like whipped cream.

The man at the stern was flung back across his seat by the sudden force, and Purple Face lost his grip on one of his oars. He fell flat on his back with his size twelve boots kicking in the air. Away went his oar like a leaf along a gutter in a downpour. The boys crammed their knuckles into their mouths and bit their lips to stop themselves from screaming with laughter – but not little Spud. She laughed herself silly at the antics of the funny men falling about.

As soon as he could, Ernie pulled himself together. Waiting until the rowing-boat was parallel with the shore, as he had done many times before while riding the whirlpool, he gave a deft double-twist with the blades. That was enough to flick the little craft out into the seaward tug of the main current.

Chapter 6

The Race for the Runaway Oar

"Quick! We've got to get after that oar," said Ernie. "You come alongside me, Edward. I'll never be able to catch up with it on my own. With the tide running like this, you never know how the current might take us."

"Me? I wouldn't be any good. I'd be useless! I've never rowed before," said Edward.

"You'll be fine, cocker," said Ernie. "It's as easy as frying an egg!"

A vision of a frying pan and two "whistlers", one a nasty mess but the other one lying perfect in the sizzling fat, came into Edward's mind. It was there for less than a second, but somehow it gave him the courage to try. He struggled up from his seat in the bow, and though the boat dipped and bucked alarmingly, he didn't lose his nerve. He clambered next to Ernie, and very soon he was pulling stroke for stroke with his experienced friend.

Futter the cox'un kept them hard at it in the chase. He pulled Florry into his lap for safety and kept a sharp eye out for the runaway oar, calling "Thar she blows!" and "Easy, Wilson!" and "Steady on your side, the chap with the cap!" and "Together, both", so that soon they got into a rhythm, and Edward felt that he'd been born to row.

They were almost down as far as the dog biscuit factory, with the sweat running into their eyes and their hands blistered, before they caught up with the runaway oar. And though it was longer than their boat, and it seemed incredibly heavy, they got it aboard somehow, and limped back with it to the steps by the bargeworks.

The rowing-boat was safely made fast to its mooring-ring. Florry was placed back in her pram on top of her clean nappy – which was still as dry as a ship's biscuit. By then the three triumphant members of the Dare Gang had decided what to do about the police boat. They could see it going round and round in the middle-distance and they could see the two policemen staggering about, trying in vain to get her restarted. The boys' idea was to run along to the Harbour Master's hut and alert him. But the fact was, with plenty of barges, coasters and pleasure-steamers passing within hailing distance, they were in no danger. In fact, there was a good chance they would be rescued any minute. So when a muffled voice, ever so posh, called, "I say, you fellows! Would you mind awfully providing some foreground for me?" they thought they could spare a minute or two to oblige a smart young photographer.

The voice of the photographer was muffled, because it came from under a thick black cloth. What the Dare Gang turned to see was a tripod of varnished wood with little black butterfly nuts at the telescoping joints. Behind it, they saw the baggy trousers of a fashionable young bloke who was training his plate-camera at the river scene, part of which, without meaning to, they had become.

Ernie and Futter and Edward began to slap their clothes to make themselves a bit smarter and Futter did his best to get his hair out of his eyes – though it fell down again straightaway afterwards. When he saw what they were doing, the photographer popped out from under his cloth and said, No, no – he wanted them just as they were. "Would one of you chaps hold up the oar for me?" he suggested. "And perhaps the chappie with the short red hair would hold the baby?"

Ernie peered into the pram and saw Florry with her eyes going very peepy. He said that he thought it would be best not to disturb her, but he pulled the pram across to be in the picture. The photographer suggested that all the boys put their arms round one another's shoulders. But then he said to Edward that it would make a better composition if he got down on one knee in front of the others.

"That's it, pull your cap round straight," he said. "Now watch the birdy – and stay quite still – and – just one more." The man flipped back the black cloth, slid out his big square photographic plate, reversed it, and slid it back before ducking under his cloth once more. The boys were very, very serious. Two of them had never had their photographs taken before and didn't quite know what to expect. Edward was feeling ... strange, as though somehow this had all happened to him before.

And as for the baby – nobody noticed the big smile on her face. After all, she was out of sight, lying flat on her back. But she was looking *very* pleased with herself, and only Edward, who was kneeling quite close to her, could see what it was that made Florry smile her spuddy little smile before she fell into a contented sleep.

Maybe it was the full bottle of milk and all the excitement that made her pee six or eight inches into the air, like a little fountain, all over the nice dry nappy that Ernie had folded neatly underneath her.

"Amazing!" Edward thought. "I bet that's a record for a girl!"

Before the boys went, the man thanked them and said that if they came back tomorrow, he'd give them each a copy of the photograph.

"Thanks very much," Edward said.

"Not at all," said the photographer.

"Yes, ta ever so," said Futter. "I fancy seeing meself in a photo. Wait till George Fell sees it! He'll be rotten jealous he never come out with us today!"

"I thank *you*," said the photographer.

Ernie didn't say anything at all, didn't even nod to the man to thank him. The man took it well and said cheerio anyway, and the boys wandered along to the Harbour Master's hut, Ernie pushing the pram as steadily as he could over the cobbles, doing his best not to wake the baby.

"You might have said *something* to him," said Edward as they mooched along. "He was a good bloke. What's wrong with thanking somebody who does you a favour?"

"Ask Futter," was all that Ernie would say.

"He's on a sworn dare," explained Futter. "If you ever hear him say please or thank you, let me know, because I stand to gain fifteen shillings. And I get the same money if he tells people he's on a dare, 'cos that'd make it too easy."

"Fifteen shillings… That's a lot, isn't it?" Edward guessed.

"Nearly a week's wages for my dad!" said Futter.

"So how come you got him to swear to that?"

"Because me and George had to dance on a grave on a sworn dare, and he wouldn't do it!" Futter shuddered at the memory of a bad moment. "It was George's idea, that one, not mine."

"It was a sailor's grave!" said Ernie. "I done

all the other dares, fair and square, but you wouldn't catch me doing that – tarnishing the memory of a seaman!"

"Yeah, well, a dare's a dare," said Futter. "But fair play to Ernie, he's never broken his word on please and thank you – and that's been a swine to stick to, ain't it, Ernie? Mind you, he'll let himself slip, though, sooner or later!"

"I broke my promise once, when I wouldn't dance on that grave," said Ernie grimly. "I shan't do it again."

The Harbour Master was having a mug of tea when he heard about the police boat. "Dear, oh dear," he said calmly, peering through his binoculars to where the boys were pointing. "Dear, oh me, they do seem to have got themselves into a pickle."

He winked at the lads. "I'll get somebody out to them … soon as I've finished me spot of tea." He gave it a blow across the top, it being so hot.

"And you got their oar back for 'em, did you, lads? Well, I'd say that was well done. And worth a few bob, I shouldn't wonder, recovering valuable police property like that. Specially if you young heroes are prepared *to keep your lips sealed about the awkward little spot they got themselves into*... See what I'm saying?"

The Harbour Master fished out a pocketful of change and selected the biggest, shiniest silver coin Edward had ever seen. "There we are – half a crown. Seems about right. Tenpence each should do it. I'll get it back off them two coppers later – towing fee, sort of thing." He flipped the coin to Edward, who was surprised at the weight of it, and had another blow on his tea. It would take a fair while to drink, he said, being so hot, so the boys left him to it.

They stopped off at an ironmonger's to get the half crown changed into pennies. At first the man was suspicious and didn't want to give away all his change if the boys weren't buying anything. But when he saw their faces, he relented and counted ten big brown pennies, a whole fistful, into each of their three outstretched hands.

"I'll have a ha'porth of nails if you like, mister," said Futter, touched by the man's generosity, but the man said it didn't matter. They should go and put it in the Post Office, he said, save it for a rainy day.

Futter said cheerio when they got to Trinity Church, pointing out where the sailor's grave was before he went. Florry slept all the way home.

Ernie parked the pram up against the railings outside his house and looked up to see his mum standing at the window of the front room. She came outside, unsmiling, rustling down the steps in her long black dress, and looked into the pram. She leaned forward to take Florry out, then sprang up straight, wrinkling her nose.

"Stripe me pink, Ernie Wilson!" she shrieked. "Fancy leaving her nappy off like that! She's soaked *everything* now!"

Edward took cover behind a plane tree.

"I can't even trust you with the simplest task!" Ernie's mother shouted. You want a DGH, you do – a Damn Good Hiding! And what time d'you call this to come in for your tea?"

Edward's hand went to his pocket and found the watch, like a ripe plum, warm and smooth. A ripe plum. Ripe. So that was it. The time was ripe again. The sequence must be coming to an end. He tugged out the watch and looked at it.

Maybe it was the late sun glinting on the glass that dazzled him. Anyway, something was so bright, he had to snap shut his eyes to block it out. He steadied himself against the trunk of the tree and was shocked to find, when he opened his eyes, that he couldn't see anything!

He could hear the voice. That was one thing. "Never seen a mess like it! You should be ashamed of yourself!" And then he found that it wasn't the trunk of a tree he was pressing against. It was a door. A low door with a slanting top. He was in the cupboard under the stairs at Grandad Wilson's.

Chapter 7

Grandad Ducks
a Dare

....

Edward pushed open the cupboard door just
enough to see clearly. The light filtering in
from the hall picked out the row of hats to his
left – the bowler, the trilby, the topper, the
naval seaman's cap, the straw boater, the gas
mask. And there was the spare hook for the
cloth cap he was wearing. He took it off and
put it back in its place. *For next time*, he
thought.

The angry woman's voice grew louder. It
was Great Aunt Spud's, coming from the front
room. It was answered by a gruff rumbling
voice from the back room.

"Well, nobody asked you to come round
here, interfering with people!" bellowed
Grandad Wilson.

Edward pushed past the old upright Hoover,
remembering to hold the bag to stop the

spring going *tang-tang*. He stepped into the hall to listen to what was going on, closing the cupboard door silently behind him. He heard the front room furniture squeak as it was shoved about, the slap of the duster, the beat of a carpet sweeper.

"You make my blood boil!" called Aunt Spud. "I take the trouble to come round here and sort you out. I clean this house from top to bottom. And all I get is aggravation. Never a word of thanks. Not that I expect thanks."

Edward crept into the back room, where his Grandfather winked at him and put his finger to his lips. Edward understood that he was not to interrupt a game that gave these two old people a great deal of pleasure.

"Moan, moan, moan!" yelled Grandad Wilson, grinning broadly.

"And why don't you get shot of those dreadful geraniums in the hall," returned Aunt Spud. "They stink the place out!"

"We've always had geraniums in this house!" thundered Grandad Wilson. "So you're not slinging them out now. Anyway, they're Roger's favourite, aren't they, Edward?"

"Is that boy still here?" shrieked Aunt Spud, puffing a bit now as she swung the carpet sweeper up and down. "It's getting on, you know. He's going to be late home for his tea. Not that I suppose that matters these days. But when I was a kiddy, people had manners. Children knew how to behave when I was a kiddy."

"Yes, we know all about when you were a kiddy!" yelled Grandad Wilson. And he added quietly, "Don't we, cocker?" *Dink-dink* went his moustache, just on one side.

"Can I see the photo?" said Edward.

"Help yourself," said Grandad Wilson.

Edward took it off the sideboard and stared at the brown and white likenesses of young Ernie Wilson, holding the pram steady, and his friend Futter, holding the runaway oar.

"You never told me you had red hair," he said. "I somehow thought it had always been white."

"You never asked me," said Grandad Wilson. He scooped up Roger and sat down in the big armchair with a sigh. "Futter's dead, you know. Night before we left the college to join the Navy, he decided to climb the rigging of the *Fame* – for a lark. Must have lost his footing in the dark. They found him cold on the concrete in the morning. He was only fourteen."

"And you've kept your word to him all this time?" said Edward. "You've *never* said please or thank you?"

"Never."

"Don't you think you could, you know, just let it drop now?"

"That'd be dancing on his grave!" said Grandad Wilson.

"Futter wouldn't have wanted you to muck up your life over a dare," said Edward.

"A dare's a dare," said Grandad Wilson. "And besides," he went on, making his moustache twitch mischievously – *dink-dink* – just on one side, "it hasn't mucked up my life.

It's being so awkward that keeps me going! Eh, Roger?" He smoothed back the cat's ears affectionately so that Roger stood in his lap and arched his ginger back.

"That's the cap on the peg in the cupboard under the stairs, isn't it, Grandad?" said Edward, pointing to the cap that seemed to be floating in the air. But it wasn't floating, Edward knew. It was sitting firmly on the head of a Time Sailor who had no reflection, no full reality – unless the time was ripe. Edward checked the pocket of his jeans – just to be sure. Yes, the watch was there, his watch now.

"Will the watch take you anywhere back in history, Grandad?" Edward asked.

"Well ... all I know for sure is, it'll take you anywhere in my history – but only if you start from this house and you know where you're aiming."

"And does where you aim for depend on what hat you're wearing?" asked Edward.

"That's right, cocker, you've got it!

Different hat, different sequence. But I shouldn't go spreading it about!" Grandad Wilson smiled. "Or people will start saying that you're as daft as me."

"The Dare Gang never splits," said Edward. Then he said, "Shall I let you into a secret – about Aunt Spud?"

"What's that, old cocker?"

"Look here, then, at the photo. See the pram? Well, look. There's a little fountain shooting up from inside. There, look. Can you see it?"

"Well, I'm blowed!" said Grandad Wilson.

"You know what that is, don't you!"

Grandad Wilson rubbed his whiskery face. "Not my little Spuddy, surely!" he chuckled. "Never as high as that!"

"It *is!*" laughed Edward. "I know it is!"

"Well, stap me!" roared Grandad Wilson. "What a girl! She does better a squirt than Roger!"

"I dare you to tell her," said Edward.

"No fear. More than my life's worth!"

As for little Spuddy, serious Aunt Spud, clean-and-tidy, everything-in-its-place, butter-wouldn't-melt *Great* Aunt Spud: she had no idea what all the giggling was about.

She was happy enough to hear her brother and the boy having a laugh. Not that she would admit it: that wasn't her way.

He was always getting stuck with me when I was a kiddy, she thought to herself. *I suppose it's only fair that I should be looking after him now. After all, I know how to sort him out.*

And she knocked a cushion into shape with two powerful left jabs.

Doof! Doof!

MORE WALKER RACERS

For You to Enjoy

☐ 0-7445-4302-9   *Creepe Hall*
by Alan Durant/Hunt Emerson   £3.99

☐ 0-7445-6012-8   *The Curse of the Skull*
by June Crebbin/Derek Brazell   £3.99

☐ 0-7445-6032-2   *Bernard's Gang*
by Dick Cate/Scoular Anderson   £3.99

☐ 0-7445-6047-0   *Jeremy Brown and the
Mummy's Curse*
by Simon Cheshire/
Hunt Emerson   £3.99

☐ 0-7445-6025-X   *Seven Weird Days at Number 31*
by Judy Allen/Derek Brazell   £3.99

☐ 0-7445-5223-0   *Smart Girls*
by Robert Leeson/Axel Scheffler   £3.99

☐ 0-7445-6018-7   *The Supreme Dream Machine*
by Jon Blake/Paul Sample   £3.99

☐ 0-7445-6303-8   *Pure Chance*
by Gillian Rubenstein/
Caroline Binch   £3.99

Name _____

Address _____

_____